GOING FOR
THE GOLD

GOING FOR THE GOLD

THE GOLD

BY PERDITA FINN

SCHOLASTIC INC.

New York   Toronto   London   Auckland   Sydney
Mexico City   New Delhi   Hong Kong   Buenos Aires

ISBN-13: 978-0-439-89208-7
ISBN-10: 0-439-89208-2

12 11 10 9 8 7 6 5 4 3 2 1   7 8 9 10 11 12/0

Printed in the U.S.A.
First printing, November 2007

Cover and chapter opener illustrations by Brandon Dorman
Additional illustrations by Mike Moran

For Joshua and Gillian,
great athletes, ancient friends

GOING FOR
THE GOLD

1 ON YOUR MARKS . . .

"I don't know what you're so upset about," said Mrs. Lexington, looking at Josh's report card. "There's nothing wrong with a B."

"A B in gym, Mom!" moaned Josh, shaking his head with disbelief. "I've never gotten a B in gym."

"I got a B minus," said Katie. "You don't see me throwing a fit."

"Yeah," said Josh, "but you're a girl. You're not supposed to be good at gym."

"Joshua Lexington!" exclaimed his mother. "Your sister is an excellent athlete. Didn't she get the soccer award last year for most valuable player?"

"Then how come she got a B minus?" asked Josh.

"The same reason you got a B," said Katie. "Because Mr. Kilmer is the most insane, out-of-control gym teacher ever. I talked while he was taking attendance one day, and he's had it in for me ever since."

Mrs. Lexington sighed and took out some magnets to post the children's report cards on the refrigerator. All year long, she'd been hearing stories about Mr. Kilmer, the new physical education teacher at Alice R. Quigley Middle School. One parent had complained when he started making the kids do push-ups if they were even a minute late for class. Another had called the school after Kilmer had made the children run more than a mile. "I'm sure nobody got an A." Mrs. Lexington tried to comfort Josh, who sat with his head in his hands at the kitchen table.

"I don't think anybody did," said Katie. She started setting the table for dinner. "He's always telling us, 'There's not a one of you who knows how to win. You're not tough enough. You're too scared of pain.'"

"Yeah," said Josh. He rubbed his leg where he'd been hit earlier in the day with a dodgeball. "Killer Kilmer's into pain."

"He thinks our school won't win the Winter Games against Morris Middle School at the end of the month," Katie added.

"Well, he's right," said Josh miserably. "We won't. We don't have enough fast kids for the running races and we'll get creamed in dodgeball. We always do."

At dinner, the kids were still talking about the upcoming competition.

"The thing is," said Josh, passing his father the potatoes, "Morris Middle School has this new sixth grader who's amazing. I saw him on the soccer field. He's like lightning. He's going to win everything — the races, the tug-of-war. And he'll destroy us in dodgeball. This kid can do backflips and kick a ball!"

"I remember hearing about that boy," said Katie. "What was his name?"

"Something weird," said Josh. "Hippo-something."

3

"Hippolytus!" Katie remembered. "Kids still talk about him. He's like a superhero or something. We'll never win."

"The important thing, kids," interrupted Mr. Lexington, "is that you have fun. It's not all about winning. How often have I said that to you?"

"Tell that to Mr. Kilmer," Katie groaned.

"I just wish we had a kid like that at our school," said Josh, sighing. "Then we could win and maybe Kilmer would lay off the rest of us."

Suddenly, Katie had a thrilling idea — an idea so exciting she didn't finish her dinner, skipped dessert, and raced through her homework. And then she tapped her foot impatiently while she waited for Josh to finish his, so she could drag him upstairs to her room to tell him what it was.

She slammed the door shut and shoved her brother down onto her desk chair. "Listen," she whispered. "I know where to find that kid."

"Quit pushing me around," said Josh. "What kid?"

"The superathlete. The one who's going to play for Alice R. Quigley in the Winter Games and beat that kid with the weird name from Morris Middle School."

"Okay, I'm listening," said Josh. He knew his sister. She actually could come up with some pretty sneaky plans. "Where's he going to come from?"

Katie took a deep breath and smiled. "Time Flyers."

Josh gasped.

Time Flyers was a student-exchange program Mrs. Lexington had signed the family up with at the beginning of the year. The kids, who came for a short stay each month, were from different countries. And from different centuries . . . only Mr. and Mrs. Lexington didn't know about the time-travel part. Nobody did. That was Josh and Katie's secret.

"But we don't have any say in who comes," said Josh. "I mean, we don't even know when they're arriving, much less who they are or what part of history they're from."

"I think we should ask this time," said Katie. "We deserve something after everything we've put up with this year."

"But how do we get in touch with Mr. Dee?" asked Josh. Mr. Dee was the mysterious director of the program, whom they had never met.

"The same way we have in the past," said Katie. She shook her head. Sometimes her brother could be so dumb. "We'll e-mail him."

They checked to make sure their mother was busy downstairs and snuck into her office. Quickly, Katie opened the Time Flyers Web site and pulled up Mr. Dee's e-mail address. She turned to her brother. "What kind of kid should we ask for?"

"A ninja," said Josh immediately. "You know, a superhero type with special powers. *Wham! Bam!*" Josh started punching his fists in the air and doing karate kicks.

"Sssh!" said Katie. "Mom'll hear us and wonder what we're up to." She began typing. "*Dear Mr. Dee,*" Katie read aloud. "*We were wondering if maybe this time you could send us a kid who is really, really good at sports.*"

"No!" said Josh. "Say ninja. We want a ninja."

"*Whoever it is,*" wrote Katie deliberately, "*just

make sure they are super-tough and strong and fast." Katie stopped typing and turned to Josh. "It doesn't matter where the kid is from. We just want a good athlete, right?"

"I guess," said Josh, sighing. He really wanted a ninja.

Katie clicked SEND and leaned back in her chair. "I wonder how long we'll have to wait for an answer?"

"Not long!" said Josh. "Look!" An IM had appeared almost at once on the screen.

All taken care of, it read. *No need to worry.*

"I wish he hadn't said that," said Katie, biting her lip.

"Why?"

" 'Cause now I'm worried."

The next morning, Katie and Josh woke up to a world covered in snow. "No school," said Mrs. Lexington when they came downstairs for breakfast.

"And no work for me until I dig out that driveway," Mr. Lexington said as he poured himself another cup of coffee.

"Oh, yes. We better get to that," agreed Mrs. Lexington. "We've got a Time Flyer arriving today."

"We do?" Despite the instant messages from the night before, Josh and Katie were surprised. They thought it might take weeks.

"Yes," said their mother. "I had such a nice e-mail from Mr. Dee last night. He told me we could expect Leonidas this morning. He's from Greece. Isn't that interesting?"

"Greece?" said Josh. "I wanted a ninja. What are Greeks good at?"

"Joshua Lexington!" said his mother. "We will welcome every child who comes to our house."

"I'm just glad to know when the boy's coming," said Mr. Lexington. "Finally, that wacky program is getting a little more organized." Usually, their Time Flyers arrived *very* unexpectedly.

"Greece!" muttered Josh. He put on his mittens a few minutes later, so he could help dig out the driveway. "I told you to ask for a ninja."

"You are so thick sometimes," said Katie,

bundling up beside him. "What is ancient Greece famous for?"

Josh thought. "Gods and goddesses, old ruins..." He stopped and smiled. "Heroes, Hercules, and..." His smile grew bigger. Then he beamed at Katie and said, "The Olympics."

"That's right," agreed Katie. "The Olympics."

And just at that moment, there was a sonic boom and a flash of blue light.

2 GET SET, GO!

"What was that?" asked Mrs. Lexington, rushing out of the kitchen. The flash of blue light had blacked out the electricity, and soon the TV crackled and started smoking.

"Some kind of power surge, I think," answered Mr. Lexington, looking around. "Must be a lot of snow on the lines."

Josh and Katie looked at each other. They knew it wasn't a power surge. A Time Flyer had just arrived. The kids always came this way. But the sound effects had never been quite so startling.

"Wow!" whispered Katie to her brother. "That

was really something. I guess this one must be kind of special."

"Wonder where he is," answered Josh. He peered out the front window. Through a swirl of snow, he could just make out a flash of red down the driveway. "Look!" he pointed.

"Oh, my goodness! Is that our Time Flyer?" Mrs. Lexington turned to her husband. "Abner, I told you to get that driveway shoveled! That poor boy's ride couldn't get the car in. They must have dropped him off on the road. He'll be all wet and cold when he gets in. Kids, run out and welcome him."

But she needn't have said anything. Josh and Katie were already out the door.

"Over here!" Katie shouted through the snow as the red-clad figure approached.

"I'm Josh!" said her brother, running up to the new kid and slapping him on the shoulder. The red cape he wore was wrapped around his head and body. Josh grabbed him by the cloak and guided him toward the house.

"Don't tell our parents you're from the past," Katie yelled over the roaring wind.

"They don't know anything about the program," added Josh. "Don't worry. We'll cover for you!"

"I hear and will obey," said the boy. His voice was surprisingly deep and smooth.

Katie opened the door. "C'mon in and get warm."

"Hello! Hello!" trilled Mrs. Lexington from the kitchen. "The electricity's back, and I'm heating some cocoa to warm you up! I'll be out to say hello in a minute."

The boy shook the snow from his shoulders. "All hail, children of Abner and Betsy of Lexington. I am Leonidas of Sparta."

The boy stood ramrod-straight and raised his right arm as if in salute. He threw the hood off his face, revealing a chiseled profile and a mane of long, curly black hair that fell almost to his waist. But Josh and Katie weren't looking at his hair.

"Oh, no!" said Katie.

"Not another one!" groaned Josh.

"Oh, my!" said Mr. Lexington, coming into the hallway to meet their newest guest.

Underneath his cloak the boy wasn't wearing anything except for the Time Flyers hourglass necklace that somehow allowed the kids to time travel. But other than that — nothing. Not even shoes. Not even underwear.

"Cover yourself up," said Josh as soon as he'd collected himself. They'd had a kid arrive naked once before, so Josh wasn't completely freaked out by this. But he grabbed hold of the boy's cloak and pulled it shut around his front quickly.

"Well, young man, I guess you're used to warmer weather in Greece," coughed a flustered Mr. Lexington. "Better get your luggage and put something a little warmer on."

The boy looked at him steadily. "I am not cold. I have no need of warmth." Despite his words, his lips did look a little blue and he was shivering ever so slightly.

"Really?" said Mr. Lexington nervously. "I'm pretty glad I've got my long underwear on."

"Yup," interrupted Josh. "That's what you

13

need. Underwear. Upstairs to my room." At this point, Josh was used to lending out his clothes to strange kids from the past. Josh grabbed Leonidas by the arm and started to drag him upstairs.

Katie watched them go, a strange, glazed expression on her face. "I haven't introduced myself yet. I'm Katie. Katie Lexington. I live here." She turned bright red and held out her hand for him to shake as he passed her.

He ignored it but bowed his head ever so slightly. "Demetrius has spoken to me of your accomplishments, Kate, daughter of Abner. He said you are a maid worthy of Sparta."

Katie blushed an even brighter red than the boy's cloak and didn't say anything.

Josh looked at his sister, surprised, and pulled the new kid upstairs.

"All right," he said, once they were in his room and the door was shut. "Here are jeans, socks, a T-shirt, a polar fleece . . . oh, and some underwear. This is the uniform of the future."

Leonidas studied the clothes that Josh had placed on the lower bunk without saying a word.

He picked the polar fleece up and rubbed the cloth between his fingers. Then he pressed on the mattress and felt the blankets. He examined the pillows and glanced around at the shelves covered in old Lego projects and well-worn books. "This is a soft place," he finally said.

"Soft?" said Josh.

"You have many soft things in this room. The toys of a boy. The pillows of a Persian. They make a man soft. Now I see why I have been sent."

"Are you saying I'm not tough enough?" Josh bristled.

"Already I have trained many of the younger boys at the *agōgē*. We will begin with this room."

"What are you talking about? You're not here to train me. You're here to help us win the Winter Games against Morris Middle School. That's what we asked for, anyway."

Leonidas nodded his head while Josh spoke and smiled ever so slightly. "Yes, yes, Demetrius prepared me for your concerns."

"Who's Demetrius? Is that Mr. Dee?"

"He is my mentor in Sparta."

"Sparta?" said Josh. "Where's Sparta? We were supposed to get a kid from Greece who's been to the Olympics and stuff."

"I *have* competed in the Olympic Games," said Leonidas. "And I have earned an olive wreath for my *polis*. There was an Athenian boy who was famed for his speed in the races and of whom everyone spoke with awe at his power and strength, but I beat him and he disappeared without a trace. Sparta is always stronger than Athens."

"Well, good for you," said Josh. "That's what we want you to do here. Win something for us against Morris Middle."

"I hope I will have a competitor as worthy of my talents as the Athenian."

"The Morris Middle kids are pretty tough. Now put on some clothes."

"I have no need of clothes."

"*I* need you to have clothes on," said Josh, taking a big breath. "Put them on now."

Leonidas merely looked at him and did nothing. Josh tried again. "Look, I don't care if you are

16

warm or freezing, but you have to cover yourself up. We wear pants here, and if you're going to fit in, you've gotta, too."

Leonidas considered this. "It is true that I must not stand out. I am here in secret, after all. For now, I will abide by the rules of your kingdom," he agreed. "I think the stiffness of these, what do you call them — jeans — will perhaps toughen the skin on my legs."

"Whatever works," said Josh. "Let's go get some cocoa and you can meet my mom."

When the boys came into the kitchen, Mrs. Lexington was giggling with Katie at the table. "Oh, Katie, you were right!" she said when she saw Leonidas.

"Sssh! Mom! I told you not to say anything," whispered Katie.

"Hello, Leonidas. It's such a pleasure to have you with us. I've heated up some of the muffins we had for breakfast, and here's some warm cocoa. I don't know if you have cocoa in Greece, but it's the perfect drink on a chilly day."

"Betsy makes a good cup of cocoa, Leo," said Mr. Lexington. He was sitting at the table with a steaming mug.

"I thank you for your hospitality, mother and father of Kate and Joshua. But I have no need of food or drink."

"Oh," said Mrs. Lexington, taken aback. "Did you eat on the flight?"

"I did fly on the wings of Hermes, but I did not eat."

"Hermes. Hmmm. Don't know that airline," said Mr. Lexington. "I guess it's Greek to me!" He gave a hearty laugh, but Leonidas just stared at him. "Well," he said, clapping his hands. "I better get to shoveling that driveway. Any of you kids want to help me?"

"If it is labor you require, I would be honored to assist you," said Leonidas.

"I just do it 'cause it's fun to be outside," Josh muttered to Katie.

Outside, Leonidas shoveled like a madman, lifting huge mounds of snow up over his head and tossing them into a pile. He cleared most of the driveway on his own. Because he had refused to wear a coat, Katie could see the muscles rippling in his arms. "He's so strong!" she gushed to Josh.

"I'm strong, too," said Josh. "I just don't need to make a big show of it."

When they were finally finished and had gone back inside, Josh was ready to collapse on the couch and watch videos for the rest of the morning. But Leonidas stood by the couch, his arms straight by his sides, his feet slightly apart, looking skeptically at the television. "Is it time for some festival?" asked Leonidas.

"Festival?" said Josh. "No. I just thought we could rest for a bit."

"Rest?" said Leonidas. "We have not done any training today."

"Training?" asked Josh.

"Are there not Games approaching? Do we not have to beat the armies of Morris?"

"Well, yeah," answered Josh without moving.

Leonidas nodded his head and narrowed his eyes. He was looking at Josh very carefully. "I'll race you to the top of the stairs."

19

Josh somehow found himself running up and down the stairs with Leonidas for the rest of the morning. Then they wrestled, lifted some old hand weights of Mrs. Lexington's, and even did gymnastics in the living room. Leonidas was faster and stronger than Josh, and Josh became more and more determined to beat him. Katie joined them from time to time. "This is kind of fun," she said, trying to do a headstand.

"You do not have bad balance," commented Leonidas. Katie worked even harder to keep from falling down and kept checking to see if Leonidas was watching her. Josh just collapsed on the carpet after a while.

At one point, Mrs. Lexington came into the living room. "You children are staying very active today, aren't you? Is that why you ate all the muffins?"

Trying to catch his breath, Josh answered her. "I haven't had any muffins since breakfast."

"Me, neither," said Katie.

"I guess your father ate them all before he left for the office then," said Mrs. Lexington, confused. "In any case, I'll have lunch ready in a few minutes."

At lunch, Leonidas stared at his peanut-butter-and-jelly sandwich and glass of milk.

"Is this the milk of an animal?" he asked Mrs. Lexington.

"Yes, dear," she answered. "I don't much like soy milk, although I know some people drink it. Is that what you're used to in Greece?"

"I have heard that barbarians drank the milk of animals, but I never quite believed it."

"Barbarians?" said Josh. "We're not barbarians. *We* wear clothes."

Mrs. Lexington just looked startled. "Perhaps a glass of juice then, Leonidas?"

"No, thank you. I have no need of food or drink."

It was the same at dinner. "You've got to try lasagna, Leo," urged Mr. Lexington. "All of our Time Flyers love Betsy's lasagna." But Leonidas just shook his head and sat unmoving throughout the entire meal.

"He doesn't seem to eat anything," whispered

Mrs. Lexington to her husband when she and Mr. Lexington went to the kitchen to get dessert.

"I wouldn't worry too much about it, Betsy," answered Mr. Lexington. "He's an awfully fit kid. Look at the muscles on him. He's probably just feeling shy his first day here."

Mrs. Lexington carried in a tray of steaming apple crisp with vanilla ice cream, which she hoped would tempt him. "Tell us about your family, Leonidas," she said as she served it.

"My father is a great warrior, and my mother prays she has given birth to a hero," he said simply.

"Ah, a military family," said Mr. Lexington, scooping out the ice cream. "I should tell you that I once played General Washington in *Georgie, Grab Your Musket*."

Josh pretended to gag.

"Do you have any brothers or sisters?" asked Mrs. Lexington.

"None living."

"Oh, I'm sorry to hear that, dear. What happened, if you don't mind my asking?"

"Not at all. The council deemed them inferior, and they were left to die on the hill."

No one said anything. Josh and Katie exchanged startled glances. There was always the danger that a Time Flyer might say something that would reveal their secret to everybody else. "You're kidding, right?" said Josh fiercely.

"Yeah," said Katie. "I'd love to leave Josh out on a hill to die. Ha-ha-ha." She forced a laugh.

Mr. and Mrs. Lexington visibly relaxed. "I'm so sorry. I shouldn't have pried," said Mrs. Lexington, somewhat uncomfortably. "Some siblings just don't get along."

Later when they were upstairs by themselves, Katie approached Leonidas. "Did they really kill your brothers and sisters?"

"What do your people do with weak infants?"

"Um, take care of them?" said Katie.

"That is why you are a weak people. I am surprised that Josh still sleeps at home like a babe under the roof with women. But we will do what we can to strengthen him."

At that moment, Josh started to scream. "What have you done to my room?"

Leonidas smiled at Katie as Josh rushed out into the hallway. "All the blankets and both the top and bottom bunk are sopping wet. Plus the window's open and there is ice — ICE — forming in my room. Where are we going to sleep?"

"We will sleep like soldiers on the floor, Josh. Together we can endure it."

"Why do we have to?" said Josh, bewildered.

"So we can win!" Leonidas beamed.

3 OUT OF BOUNDS

The next morning, Josh took a hot shower for almost a half an hour. Not only was he freezing after sleeping on the floor with the window open in mid-January, he was sore from all the exertion the day before.

"You should have come and slept in my room," said Katie when he finally emerged from the bathroom.

"I tried to," said Josh. "But Leonidas was sleeping in front of the door. Every time I went to step over him, he'd grab me by the ankle and tell me to go back to sleep. I told you we should have asked for a ninja."

"But you've got to admit, he's pretty amazing. Like a Greek god," said Katie. "Where is he?"

"I don't know. He got up hours ago. I hope he's gone."

But Leonidas was sitting in the kitchen with their mother. "Leo has just been reciting the whole story of the Trojan War for me," she explained to Josh and Katie. "It's been absolutely thrilling. Did you know that Helen, the most beautiful woman in the whole world, was from Sparta? That's Leo's hometown. By the way, Josh, did you do something with all the bread? I can't find any to make your sandwiches for school."

"I didn't touch it, Mom," said Josh. "But I don't mind buying lunch today. It's pizza."

On the way to school, Leonidas marveled not only at the speed of the car but the metal and hard plastic it was made with. "With such a shield, an army would be invincible in battle," he commented to Josh. "It would be better than the Trojan horse."

"Tanks," bragged Josh. "Our armies have these metal cars called tanks."

"Yeah," said Katie. "And now everybody has bombs that blow them up."

"What are bombs?" asked Leonidas eagerly.

"Secret weapons," said Katie.

"You're going to be *our* secret weapon," said Josh. "I can't wait until Kilmer meets you. Then he'll realize we can win the Winter Games and lay off the rest of us."

After signing in, Leonidas joined Josh in Mrs. Pitney's class. All morning, he struggled to sit still and had a terrible time paying attention. He looked out the window and wriggled in his seat and once even stood up and started jumping up and down.

"What are you doing, young man?" asked Mrs. Pitney, aghast.

"I'm not used to being so still. When do we begin training?"

"Gym is next," whispered Josh. "Sit down."

Leonidas sighed. "I don't know, Josh," he said in the hall. "Taught by women, sleeping under the same roof as women . . . no wonder you are useless in competition."

"Let's just go to gym," said Josh with a shrug. "I think you'll like Mr. Kilmer."

In the locker room, Josh pulled out the extra T-shirt and pair of shorts that he had brought for Leonidas, but the boy had disappeared. "Hey," Josh said to his best friend, Neil Carmody. "Have you seen the new kid? He was just beside me."

"Yeah," stammered Neil. "He just walked out into the gym. I can't believe it. I mean, wow."

All at once Josh heard hoots of laughter. It could only mean one thing. He rushed out through the locker room doors into the gym. It was just as he'd suspected. Leonidas was standing without any clothes on in the middle of the gymnasium.

Boys and girls were pointing and hollering, but Leonidas just stood there, absolutely straight and unashamed. He seemed to be examining the climbing ropes suspended from the ceiling. "Get back in here!" Josh shouted to him. But he was too late. Mr. Kilmer had seen Leonidas, and his gaze was locked on the new kid's feet.

When Mr. Kilmer got angry, the veins on his thick red neck bulged out and pulsed. They were throbbing now as he shouted across the room. "Where are your sneakers, boy? No one, absolutely no one, comes into my gym without sneakers. That includes you, Joshua Lexington." Kilmer's face was red, the stiff hair of his crew cut stood straight up, and his enormous muscles tightened.

"What about his gym shorts, Mr. K.? Doesn't he need those, too?" shouted Frank Lubka.

Mr. Kilmer looked up from Leonidas's bare feet and jumped back. "Holy gamoley, boy! What are you doing out here in your birthday suit?" He dropped his clipboard in disbelief. The class burst out laughing again. "Get back in the locker room right this minute." Mr. Kilmer pushed a surprised Leonidas back through the doors.

"What do you think Kilmer will do to him?" asked Evan Ferrante.

"Make him do ten thousand push-ups at least," guessed Neil, "if he comes out alive."

"If," said Josh. He wondered if he should go into the locker room and try and protect Leonidas, but he'd probably make everything worse. Besides,

Leonidas seemed like someone who could take care of himself in these kinds of situations.

"Your new friend is quite the show-off," said a snide voice. It was Lizzie Markle, the most popular, and the most difficult, girl in the whole sixth grade — and the only one who'd figured out there was something strange going on with the Lexingtons' foreign exchange students.

"But he's kind of cute," added Vanessa, Lizzie's best friend. "From what I saw of him."

"Which was everything," said Lizzie. "Where's he from?"

But before Josh could answer, Leonidas and Mr. Kilmer reappeared. Leonidas was now wearing gym shorts, a T-shirt, and sneakers. Kids immediately crowded around him. "What did he do to you, huh?"

"Is he gonna flunk you?"

"How many push-ups did he give you?"

Leonidas brushed them off. "I deserved a flogging for not anticipating his rules, but he merely whipped me with words."

Mr. Kilmer strode over to Josh. "Lexington,

I'm holding you responsible for these shenanigans. You're hosting this foreigner. I want ten push-ups, right now. Drop, sir."

"Why me?" asked Josh. "It was his fault. He just admitted it."

"The kid's from another country. What does he know? Says that's the way they work out where he comes from. And it makes a certain kind of sense. You should have prepared him. Make it fifteen on the double. And when you're done, get yourself dressed. I'm docking you a grade today for inappropriate attire."

Josh realized too late that with all the hubbub, he hadn't changed into his own gym clothes.

By the time Mr. Kilmer had settled the class down and taken attendance, it was almost time to go. Instead of the dodgeball game they were supposed to play, Mr. Kilmer had them run around the gym. "Faster, faster. They got a new kid at Morris Middle School who can outrace a car, and no one here could even beat an out-of-shape slug," he shouted as they trotted passed him. None of the kids really listened. They were used to his shouting. Some kids walked, others managed to dash around once or twice before settling into a slow jog, and a few gasped for breath. Leonidas ran laps around them all, but Mr. Kilmer was so busy putting marks in his record book he didn't seem to notice.

When Mr. Kilmer blew his whistle for them to stop, Leonidas shook his head. "That's it?"

"Yeah, that was brutal," said Josh.

"Brutal? Why, such a master as this wouldn't be fit to train the suckling babes in Sparta."

"Ssh! If you're talking, Kilmer takes off more points. Now he's got to yell at us about the Winter Games. I'm surprised he didn't say anything about your running. I don't know if he's realized yet what a difference you're going to make to our team."

"How could he?" said Leonidas. "We didn't do anything." He looked around the room. "I must say, Josh, we have our work cut out for us. Your master is doing nothing to prepare any of you."

"Nothing?" said Josh. "We just ran like almost

a mile! And I did fifteen push-ups, no thanks to you."

"All right, class," boomed Mr. Kilmer. "Listen up, you lazy snails! As some of you may remember, we've got the Winter Games coming up. Quigley Middle School's very own Olympics is what I like to think of them as, and we can't worry about a little pain when we're getting ready. I want you all to show up tomorrow ready to work, work, work. I want you to start really pushing yourselves. And I want you all in your gym clothes. No naked kids. Do you hear me?"

"Yes, Mr. Kilmer," they all groaned.

"All right, then. Class dismissed."

In the locker room, Leonidas couldn't believe they had to change back into their school clothes. "We are headed back into that room to sit and do nothing again?" he asked, horrified.

"Not nothing," said Josh. "We've got math."

"By Zeus, my limbs will wither away with disuse!" moaned Leonidas. "How can we sit and sit and sit and move our bodies so little?"

"You get to stand up during chorus," added Neil.

"Chorus?" said Leonidas. "You actually sing in these barbarian lands?"

"You like singing?" asked Josh, surprised.

"Men who can sing together can fight together," said Leonidas.

"I never thought of it that way," said Josh. "And I'm sure Mr. Kilmer never has, either."

4 LEARNING THE ROPES

"Where's your brother?" said Mrs. Lexington to Katie when she came home after getting off the bus.

"Leonidas made him get off at the first stop. He said he was tired of sitting still and they could run home together."

"It's over a mile — and there's snow on the ground!" said Mrs. Lexington.

"Josh can handle it," said Katie. "It's probably good for him. I even saw another kid running outside through the snow. Never saw him before. He must go to Morris Middle. He looked really tough. I wonder if it was that Hippolytus kid?"

Almost an hour later, the two boys burst

through the front door. Josh was red-faced and out of breath. Leonidas was exhilarated. "Training in this cold air is exciting. I was not prepared for how difficult it would be. If only I could have convinced Josh to go barefoot with me."

"Leonidas! Your feet," exclaimed Mrs. Lexington. They were red and swollen and blotched with white spots where the circulation had stopped. "You'll get frostbite. You have to wear shoes. If you don't, you're not going outside again. That's an order, young man."

Leonidas looked at Mrs. Lexington. "I will obey," he said. His eyes sparkled. "Your mother would make a great general," he later told Katie when Mrs. Lexington had left the room to go work in her office.

"But not Mr. Kilmer?" she asked.

Leonidas shook his head. "That man is all words and no action. I would be surprised if he had ever seen battle."

"He sure acts like he was in the Marines," said

Josh, sipping cocoa and warming his hands on the hot mug.

"I know not this army, but I know his kind of warrior. All bluster."

"Wait until you see him in action tomorrow. We barely had class today because of what you did."

The next day, Leonidas struggled to sit through the morning lessons and gratefully leaped out of his seat when it was time for gym. Reluctantly, he changed into gym clothes.

"C'mon!" said Josh. "Kilmer's shouting for us. It's dodgeball today."

Out in the gym, Frank and Evan were already picking teams. Josh was one of the first kids chosen; everyone knew he was a good thrower. Lizzie Markle got chosen early, too. But Leonidas was one of the last kids picked. "Oh, no! I'm stuck with Naked Kid," groaned Evan.

Mr. Kilmer faced the two teams. "This is a game about endurance, about who can take the pain and make the gain. I don't want anyone complaining or going to the nurse, you hear me? And no bathroom breaks."

"I can endure any beating," said Leonidas. "I am ready."

"You don't know what pain is, kid. I could tell you a thing or two about pain," said Kilmer.

"Do we line up against the wall and beat one another unconscious?" asked Leonidas.

Mr. Kilmer looked stunned. "What are you talking about?"

"Next year, I will participate in the whippings, and I am ready to bleed on the altar of Artemis," said Leonidas. "I will not die. I will not pass out. I will endure the lashings with strength and courage."

Mr. Kilmer gave him a strange look. "Cool it, kid. You're going freaky on me."

"You don't have to do that here," Josh shouted to Leonidas as they took their places on their separate teams. "In dodgeball, there are two teams and a bunch of balls in the middle." He pointed to the balls lined up across the gym floor.

"You run for the balls and then hurl them at kids on the other team to get them out. Last one standing wins for his team. There's no bleeding, okay?"

"I love battle ball!" said Leonidas. His eyes gleamed.

"You've played this before?" asked Josh, worried.

"Many, many times," said Leonidas. "It is excellent training for warfare. But these balls you use are most interesting." He picked up one of the red balls and studied it. "What kind of animal bladder are they made from?"

Before Josh could answer, Kilmer had blown his whistle and the ball flew out of Leonidas's hands and slammed into Josh's shoulder. "Ouch! No fair!" screamed Josh.

"You're out, Lexington!" shouted Mr. Kilmer, making a mark in his grade book.

From the sidelines, Josh watched the fastest game of dodgeball he had ever seen. One after another, kids were struck out either by Leonidas or, on the other team, by Lizzie Markle. They were both ruthless shots. Kids left the court holding on to bruised arms and rubbing rising welts on their legs. "Man, Naked Kid throws hard," said Frank, staring at Leonidas. Red gym balls ricocheted off the walls. Finally, the only two players left were Lizzie and Leonidas. They raced for balls, hurled them at each other, and managed to dash back and forth across the gym. The girls were cheering for Lizzie, and the boys started to egg on Leonidas.

"Don't let a girl beat you, Naked Kid," yelled Frank.

"Throw hard. She can take it," screamed Neil. He was no fan of Lizzie Markle's.

Even Mr. Kilmer started to join in. "C'mon, Markle! Show this class what an A in physical education really looks like."

"She got an A in gym?" said Josh to Neil, stunned.

"You didn't know that?" answered Neil.

Josh shook his head and looked back at the

game. "Go get her, Leonidas! Hit her with all you've got!"

On and on went the game — neither competitor showed signs of tiring. Leonidas whipped ball after ball across the line. Lizzie nearly caught him at one point with a carefully placed throw, but he arched his back and just avoided getting hit. "Almost!" shouted Mr. Kilmer. "Good throw, Markle! Go get him!"

"Isn't it time to go, Mr. Kilmer?" asked Vanessa, looking at the clock.

"Yeah," agreed Frank. "Gym's over."

"Don't say anything!" whispered Evan. "Maybe we can miss math."

Mr. Kilmer had dropped his clipboard and clenched his fists. He glanced at the clock and sighed through gritted teeth. He gave one quick blow on his whistle and yelled, "Freeze, both of you. It's time for Sudden Death!"

Leonidas froze and narrowed his eyes. Lizzie bent over, her hands on her knees, and caught her breath. Mr. Kilmer walked into the center of the gym with a single red ball in his hands. He placed it on the floor between Leonidas and Lizzie.

"Listen up. I'm going to count to three and blow my whistle. This is the only ball that counts now."

The next class was coming into the gym from the locker rooms. Katie appeared next to Josh. "What's happening?" she asked.

"Sudden Death. It's Leonidas against Lizzie!"

"Go, Leo!" shouted Katie.

Mr. Kilmer raised his large hand, a single finger pointing in the air. "ONE!" he yelled. Leo crouched over. Lizzie looked at Mr. Kilmer. He winked at her. She nodded. Mr. Kilmer pointed a second finger into the air. "TWO!" he yelled. He nodded at Lizzie, shouted, "THREE!" and Lizzie lunged for the ball.

"No fair!" shouted Josh and Neil. "She cheated!"

But it didn't matter. Leonidas was faster than she was. The ball was already in his hands, and he whipped it toward her as hard as he could. At such close range, it hit her right on the forehead and knocked her backward.

"Markle's down!" shouted Frank.

One of Katie's classmates pointed at Leonidas. "Who is that kid? He's gorgeous!"

"That's Leonidas. He lives at my house. He's from Greece."

"Wow!"

Mr. Kilmer was furious. He marched over to Leonidas and grabbed him by the collar. "You didn't wait until I blew the whistle. I'm disqualifying you. That's an F for gym today. Plus you hit a girl in the head."

"Kilmer said he was counting to three!" exclaimed Frank.

"He always counts to three!" added Laurie. All over the gym, kids were whispering about what had happened.

Neil spoke up. "It's no fair, Mr. Kilmer. Lizzie was already cheating. She always does."

Kilmer glared at him. "That's an F for you, too, Carmody." He made a mark on his clipboard. "We follow the rules in this class," he said to Leonidas.

"What kind of kid are you, anyway, that can't follow the rules? Give me ten push-ups."

Leonidas stared at him and the corners of his mouth crinkled into a smile. "I will give you fifty." He dropped to the floor and began effortlessly executing push-up after push-up.

"All right, kid, stop showing off," Kilmer snapped. "Everybody to class. If you're late, it's your own fault. Remember that."

Lizzie Markle was still sitting on the floor, rubbing her forehead. Leonidas came over to her and offered to help her up. "You are a worthy competitor," he said, grinning at her.

"Hmmpf," snorted Lizzie, taking his hand and pulling herself up. "At least I don't cheat."

Leonidas laughed out loud for the first time. He looked more handsome than ever with his long black hair and flashing white teeth. "No," he agreed, raising a single eyebrow. "You don't cheat. But you win. You are a winner, are you not?"

"Sometimes," acknowledged Lizzie. "Not today."

Leonidas laughed again. "I think together we can figure out how to take the prize at these Winter Games. What do you think?"

"I don't know," said Lizzie, walking away from him toward the locker room. "We'll have to talk." But she flashed him an enormous smile.

5 TIME OUT

"Kids, I need to talk with you about something serious," said Mr. Lexington when he came home from the office that night.

"What is it?" said Josh. He was showing Leonidas how to set the table.

"C'mon in here, Katie. You, too, Betsy." Everyone pulled up a seat at the dining room table. Mr. Lexington looked grim.

"The police came by just after you kids left for school this morning. It looks like there's a burglar in the neighborhood."

"Oh, Abner! How frightening!" exclaimed Mrs. Lexington. She reached out and touched

Katie's arm reassuringly. "Whose house has been robbed?"

Mr. Lexington looked grim. "Maybe ours."

"No!"

"Yes," nodded Mr. Lexington. "Remember those muffins you said I ate? And the missing bread? This thief takes food from houses in the neighborhood."

"All the potato chips were gone when I got up this morning, too!" said Mrs. Lexington. "It's so strange."

"It is, isn't it? The police said they've never seen anything like it before. Leaves the TVs, leaves the computers, and takes the pretzels. He also stole all of Mrs. Kazantziki's homemade baklava."

"What's baklava?" asked Josh.

"Greek pastry," whispered Katie.

"Oh!" said Josh. He was beginning to get the picture.

"Do you think we should be frightened, Abner?"

"I don't know, Betsy. But I do think we all need to be extra careful about locking the doors. This fellow may be a little deranged. The police actually caught sight of him this morning coming out of Mrs. Kazantziki's house. He was running through backyards as fast as lightning, but he wasn't wearing a stitch of clothing. Imagine. Stark naked in this weather."

"Oh, boy!" whispered Josh to Katie. He hoped his father wouldn't remember how Leonidas had arrived at their house.

Leonidas was nodding his head very seriously the whole time Mr. Lexington was talking. "This is most upsetting," he said calmly.

"I'm so sorry this had to happen while you were visiting," said Mrs. Lexington. "I can't remember anything so frightening in our community. I hope you won't think less of us."

"That is not possible." Leonidas smiled at Mrs. Lexington.

Later that night after dinner, up in Katie's room — Josh's room was much too cold to sit in these days — Josh and Katie grilled Leonidas.

"It's you, isn't it?" said Josh.

"It has to be," said Katie. "Who else runs naked in the snow? Who else doesn't ever eat anything at meals?"

"Who else stashed six bags of potato chips in my closet?" said Josh.

"Let me tell you what's going to happen if you get caught," said Katie. Leonidas raised an eyebrow.

"Yeah, I know you're crazy fast, but you might get caught," said Josh.

"And if you do, the police will find out that you have no passport, and they'll start investigating," said Katie.

"And we nearly got caught by Immigration in November. It was no picnic, let me tell you," added Josh, remembering an unpleasant scene with their Pilgrim Time Flyer.

"Can I tell *you* something?" Leonidas was sitting cross-legged on the floor. His back was perfectly straight as always, and despite being harangued by Katie and Josh, he seemed completely relaxed.

"Please," said Katie.

"Back in Sparta, there was a boy a few years older than me who was once accused of stealing a fox. The boy had, in fact, actually stolen the fox and had hidden it beneath his cloak. He planned to kill it, skin it, and eat it. Like most of us, he was always hungry. We are expected to steal our food. But rather than confess his crime, he held that fox against his belly and endured the soldiers' questions in silence. Finally, as they turned to go, the boy collapsed on the ground. He was dead. While he was standing there, the fox had eaten out his innards, but the boy had made no noise as he died. That boy was a warrior. He is a hero to us."

"What are you talking about?" said Josh, horrified. "What do they do to you back in Sparta? Beat you? Starve you? Kill you? Why?"

Leonidas looked confused. "How else do you train a warrior?"

"Do you get to choose?" asked Katie.

"Choose?" said Leonidas.

"Yeah. Do you get to choose what you want to be when you grow up? I mean, if you don't want to be a soldier, can you choose to be an artist or a musician or a doctor or a farmer or whatever?"

"Why would I want to be a farmer and a slave? And I would certainly not want my family's honor to be dirtied by touching money," said Leonidas. "To be a warrior is the greatest honor. I was born to it."

"Yikes!" said Josh. "I'm glad I wasn't."

"Me, too," said Katie.

Leonidas considered them both. "Neither of you would have done well in Sparta. It is true. But that girl I competed against today, that Markle, she has the heart of a champion. She is a winner."

"She's a force to be reckoned with. That's for sure," said Josh.

"She's trouble," said Katie. "Stay away from her."

Leonidas stood up and began to pace back and forth. "You requested that I come to help you win your Winter Games. Is that not right?"

"Yeah, and you will," said Josh. "You'll destroy them."

Leonidas stopped and stared at Josh. "How

can one man win against an army? In battle, you must be united, you must be an unstoppable, synchronized force. Today, I did not win at your battle ball. I lost all of my teammates. All of them. That is no triumph. If we are to truly win at your Games, every boy and girl must be at his or her optimum potential."

"Look, Leonidas," said Katie. "If Kilmer can't get kids to work out, how are you going to?"

"Yeah," said Josh. "No whipping and starvation allowed."

"That has indeed concerned me, but when I saw Lizzie play today, I realized that you Americans have it in you to win. I had begun to think you were all soft like the Athenians who must always call on us for help to win their wars."

"I thought you said the toughest kid you ever competed against was an Athenian," said Josh, remembering their earlier conversation.

"That boy was different. He was like a god. No, you are like the Athenians because you want to make decisions, *choices* as you call them. That will be the key, I think. This idea of choice. You and your classmates will be ready, Josh. I can assure you, we will win."

"If you can train everybody, right?" said Katie.

"If?" answered Leonidas.

"Kids, I've got dessert," yelled Mrs. Lexington from the bottom of the stairs.

"Please come and eat some," pleaded Katie, getting up. "So they don't suspect anything."

"And no more naked morning runs," said Josh.

"Yeah," said Katie. "You promised Mom."

"I promised your mother that I would wear shoes. And I will."

6 DRAFT PICKS

Leonidas did not sit with Josh on the bus the next morning. He took a seat in the back with Evan and Frank. "What's he want with those goons?" Neil asked Josh.

Josh just shook his head. But two stops before school, both boys followed Leonidas off the bus. "Wait a minute. Where are you going?" asked the driver.

"School," Leonidas answered and hopped off, dragging Evan and Frank with him before the driver could respond.

The next thing Josh knew, all three boys were running alongside the bus on the sidewalk, their heavy packs slapping against their backs. At each stop, they would sprint to catch up. And they arrived red-faced and out of breath at school just as Josh and Neil got off the bus. "Am I good enough, huh? You think I can do it?" Josh overheard Evan saying to Leonidas, who didn't even seem to have broken a sweat.

Leonidas looked him over from head to toe. "I am still not sure. I will have to observe you more before I decide. Remain vigilant."

"What's going on?" asked Neil.

Leonidas raised a finger to his lips and then leaned close and whispered something to Neil. Neil nodded his head and, later that morning, both boys disappeared from the classroom within minutes of each other — Neil to the nurse and Leonidas to the bathroom. They returned together about five minutes later, and Neil was out of breath. "Where were you?" Josh whispered to his friend.

"Can't tell." Neil shook his head. "It's a secret."

A few minutes later, Josh noticed Leonidas slipping a note to Nick Doinkle. The boy looked surprised. "Really, I can? You think so?"

Leonidas shrugged his shoulders and got out of his seat and walked over to the window. "You are worthy enough to try. Remember, tell no one," he said.

"What's going on?" Josh asked Leonidas when the boys were at their lockers before lunch.

"Going on?" said Leonidas. At that moment, a fifth grader dashed up the hallway, taking a flying leap in front of him.

"What do you think? Is that good enough?" the boy shouted back to Leonidas.

"Keep trying," said Leonidas as he strode down the hallway.

"Keep trying at what? What's going on?" asked Josh again, running after Leonidas.

By the time he got to the cafeteria, Leonidas was surrounded by a pack of boys all crowding around him. Josh watched as they followed him over to a table. "Will someone please tell me what's going on?" Josh asked Neil, who had just arrived.

"Leo didn't tell you?" said Neil.

"Tell me what?" Josh was getting angry now.

"I'm sworn to secrecy. I can't say anything. Nope, not a word." Neil was clearly bursting. He sighed. "I just can't believe you're not in. I mean, I felt sure he would have chosen you. Gotta go." He bounded over to the table with Leonidas and sat down, ignoring his lunch. In fact, none of the boys ate anything. And as soon as the cafeteria monitor opened the door to the playground, they leaped up and ran outside into the clear, crisp January air.

Josh ate lunch by himself. The only other person at the table was an overweight fifth grader whose name he didn't know. "How ya doin'?" Josh said politely.

"You didn't get in, either?"

"What?" said Josh, throwing down his sandwich. "Get into what?"

"The secret team. No one's supposed to know

about it. But everybody does," said the boy. "I'm going to work out like crazy this week. You gotta be good enough. That's what I hear. I figure with a little practice, I just might make it."

Josh slammed his lunch box shut, grabbed his coat, and headed outside. Some boys were running at top speed around the perimeter of the playground. A few others were doing chin-ups on the bars. Another group was playing dodgeball against the brick wall of the school building, slamming balls as hard as they could at one another. Josh was also surprised to see a whole gang of girls, led by Lizzie Markle, doing a complicated hip-hop dance on the blacktop. Usually on cold days, they just huddled together talking near the doorway.

Josh spotted Leonidas on the sidelines of the dodgeball game.

"You must know where he's going to throw the ball before it leaves his hands," Leonidas was saying to Neil. "And do not flinch if he hits you. You must be oblivious to pain."

"Okay, I think I got it. Let me try again," said Neil eagerly.

"Why don't I get to be on the team?" shouted Josh. He was furious. Ever since he could remember, he'd always been good at sports. He was often chosen first. He always got a trophy at the end of the season. And he could always kick or throw the ball where it was supposed to go. "How come you didn't even tell me about it? I mean, you're living at my house."

"But I thought you wanted me to win the Winter Games for you. I didn't realize you wanted to win them yourself." Leonidas lifted an eyebrow and smiled at Josh.

"You are really sneaky," said Josh.

"It is part of my training." Leonidas bowed slightly, complimented by Josh's comment. "Will you join us?"

"What do I have to do?"

"What everybody else is doing. Train every minute of the day that you can. Push yourself harder than you ever have before. Demand nothing but excellence from yourself."

"You got Evan and Frank and Neil to agree to do that? How?"

Leonidas took Josh by the arm and pulled him aside where they could talk privately. "Mr. Kilmer promised you nothing for your efforts but a letter on a piece of paper. It does not inspire you to greatness. I asked myself, why is it that we at the *agōgē* work so hard? Is it because we have no choice? No, we do have a choice. The best among us are chosen to be part of the secret police, and we work toward that goal with all our hearts. We want to be part of that elite force. It is special and secret and only the best are chosen."

"You want to be part of the secret police?"

"Oh, yes," said Leonidas. "That is why I agreed to expand my training with time travel."

"What will you have to do in the secret police?" asked Josh.

"It's secret," said Leonidas. "I will find out when I am accepted."

"But you decided to create a secret team here at Alice R. Quigley Middle School?"

"Yes, exactly," said Leonidas. "And it seems to be working. No one is on it yet, of course.

They must first prove themselves. If they triumph at the Winter Games, why, then I will accept them all."

"Brilliant," said Josh. "But why are you telling me?"

"Because you must be my second-in-command and help lead them to victory. Do you accept the commission?"

Just at that moment, Katie appeared. Her coat was off, her hair was tossed by the winter wind, and she was in a rage. "Look, Leonidas, I don't know why you chose Lizzie to head up the girls instead of me. She's just doing stupid dancing."

"There is no better conditioning than dancing," said Leonidas. "She is preparing a routine that we will teach to everyone. You will learn to move in formation and anticipate one another's rhythms. Lizzie understood this at once."

"She did?" said Katie. She was biting her lip and looking irritable.

"She did," said Leonidas briskly. "Now I must get back to training. And you should do so as well."

Katie grimaced and stomped back to where Lizzie was doing her hip-hop routine with a group of fifth- and sixth-grade girls. She stood in the back row, barely raising her arms, and slumping through the steps.

He knows a lot about battles, thought Josh before he headed over to the dodgeball game, *but I don't think he knows anything about girls.*

7 CURVE BALL
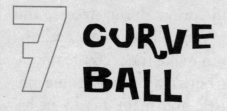

"I just can't believe it, either." Josh smiled as he listened to his mother talking on the phone. "Why, I got up this morning and Josh and Katie were already jumping rope in the living room. It's that Mr. Kilmer," she was saying. "I know we all thought he was a bit tough on the children, but I don't think Josh and Katie have turned on the television once these past two weeks. They've been too busy running around outside. I don't think Josh wants to get a B in gym again."

Josh just shook his head. He knew it wasn't Mr. Kilmer. It was Leonidas who had inspired a ragtag bunch of Xbox fanatics and DVD buffs to start flexing their muscles. Kids regularly jogged home from school now. They did stretches between classes, time trials and sprints during recess, and jumped into gym class with a brand-new enthusiasm. They all wanted to make the secret team.

Mr. Kilmer didn't know what was going on. He still blew his whistle and made marks in his grade book, but he spent a lot more time rubbing his eyes and shaking his head as if he couldn't see right. Their weekly dodgeball game had become so fierce and skillful that few kids were ever struck out — and when they were, they usually needed to go to the nurse's office for an ice pack. When they had to run around the gym, they finished so quickly the bell still hadn't rung and Mr. Kilmer didn't have anything else for them to do.

"Should we do some push-ups?" asked Frank.

"What are you talking about, Lubka?" said Mr. Kilmer.

"Can we do some push-ups?" he repeated.

"Good idea!" shouted Lizzie before Mr. Kilmer could answer. "Let's go, team." Every kid dropped to the floor.

"Are you trying to undermine my authority, Markle?" demanded Mr. Kilmer.

"Oh, no, Mr. Kilmer. We just want to win the Winter Games." Lizzie smiled at him. "You've done such a good job getting us excited about them."

Mr. Kilmer didn't look convinced, but he accepted the compliment. "I just want the rest of you to remember that doesn't mean I'm giving you all As. I grade on a curve. Remember that. I grade on a curve."

But nobody was really listening. They were doing push-ups, glancing over occasionally to make sure Leonidas was noticing how hard they were working.

"Lizzie is an excellent commander," Leonidas said to Josh as they headed back to class. "She is very clever and sneaky."

"Yeah, she's sneaky," admitted Josh, looking across the hall to where Lizzie was furtively whispering to a group of girls. "That's what worries me."

Ever since his family had been hosting Time

Flyers, Lizzie Markle had been making trouble for Josh and Katie. She had nearly ruined the play directed by their Elizabethan actor, she had almost caused their ancient Egyptian to curse Halloween, she had tried to have their visiting Pilgrim deported, and she'd just about convinced a French aristocrat to make her home in twenty-first-century America. *No*, thought Josh. *I can't believe we're going to get off easy this time.*

He watched Lizzie pass a note in class to her friend Laurie. Laurie read it, crumpled it up, dropped it on the floor, and stomped on it.

"You've got to find out what they're up to," said Josh as he and Leonidas jogged home after school. Josh was surprised to find that he no longer found it that difficult, even in the cold.

"Lizzie is very strong. Some of the girls will resent this, I am sure."

"You don't get it," said Josh. "She makes trouble. Big trouble."

When they arrived home, Katie was slumped in front of the television, a cup of cocoa in her hand. "You did not run home?" asked Leonidas, surprised.

"Nope," answered Katie. "I didn't."

"Why not?" Leonidas seemed stunned.

"No point," said Katie without looking up. "It's just a game. Who cares?"

Leonidas looked like he'd just been hit in the face with an enormous snowball. For a moment, he couldn't even speak. "Just a game?" he echoed. "Every game matters. Every game is a preparation for the ultimate battle."

"Yeah?" said Katie. "Well, good luck."

Josh was shaking his head. "What happened, sis? This isn't like you at all. Does this have something to do with Lizzie?"

"Maybe," said Katie, tight-lipped and still staring at the screen.

"You cannot let your feelings get in the way of your obedience," said Leonidas. "A good soldier knows how to follow orders without letting his emotions rule his actions."

Katie exploded. She leaped up out of her chair

and started screaming at Leonidas. "You shouldn't have picked such a snotty general, then. Do you know what Lizzie is spreading around? Do you? She is saying that she's only going to let the popular girls, her friends, be on your secret team."

"But that is what we have been telling everyone, Katie," said Leonidas. "You know that. Now everyone wants to be on the team. Because it is secret. Because it is a select group. And eventually everyone will be trained and ready. It is a trick."

"I know. And Lizzie's explained it to the girls. But she says her team really *is* going to be select. She says there is no way she's going to train everyone. You should never have picked her over me. You weren't doing a lot of thinking." Katie stormed out of the room, stomped up the stairs, and slammed the door to her room.

Leonidas looked at Josh. "I do not understand what is happening."

"You don't get girls, do you?" said Josh.

"All the girls will be trained just as all the boys will. We will win the Winter Games. What else will matter?"

"What matters is that the girls think you are the hottest guy in the whole school — and you chose one girl over all the rest. That's what matters."

Leonidas looked confused and then slowly, very slowly, Josh watched as he began to understand. "How could I not see it?" he finally moaned. "This is precisely the trap Paris fell into."

"Who?" said Josh.

"Paris of Troy. Three goddesses came to him and asked him to decide which one was the most beautiful. The two he did not choose became very angry and, the next thing you know, he had the Trojan War on his hands."

"Yup, that's what you did when you picked Lizzie to lead the girls. All the rest think you chose her because you like her more. Now we've just got to avoid a ten-year war. You don't want to fight my sister. You really don't. She used to bite."

"But I can't replace Lizzie. That will turn her into an angry, vengeful goddess."

"That's about right," agreed Josh.

"And without your sister's athletic ability we cannot win," sighed Leonidas.

"And I suspect more girls are going to follow my sister's lead and quit," said Josh, remembering Laurie's actions in class. "Just a hunch."

Leonidas groaned and threw himself down on the sofa. "I can see no way out of it. We must consult an oracle."

"A what?" said Josh.

"Where is your most reliable oracle?" asked Leonidas, barely listening. "If there is not one nearby, I suppose we could examine the entrails of a hawk or an owl. That is often helpful."

"What are entrails?"

"The intestines. The insides."

"You want to kill a bird? How's that going to help? What are you talking about?"

Leonidas gave a frustrated sigh. "We need an oracle, a seer, someone with access to the gods who can advise us. I'd really like to hear Apollo's thoughts on all this."

"You mean you want someone who can tell us the future and what to do?"

"Yes, that's it," said Leonidas.

"We don't really do that anymore."

"You don't try to figure out what is going to happen in the future, so you know how to behave in the present?"

"Everything's science now. The sun's just the sun, a big ball of fire. It's not some superhero riding his chariot across the sky."

Leonidas looked at Josh as if he were crazy. "No wonder you needed my help."

Just at that moment, Mrs. Lexington came into the room. "Are you boys ever going to come into the kitchen and have a snack?"

"Mrs. Lexington?"

"Yes, Leonidas."

"I am in need of an oracle."

"A what, dear?"

"I need the guidance of the heavens."

"Oh," she said. "That's easy. I've got the paper in the kitchen. Now when were you born? I was just checking out my horoscope this afternoon."

"Oh, no," moaned Josh as Leonidas followed his mother.

"Here we go," said Mrs. Lexington. She spread out the daily newspaper on the kitchen table.

Leonidas turned to Josh. "How remarkable to have such a convenient oracle. I can see there have been a few advancements in these times. But I am surprised you did not know about it, Josh."

"Aries, Aries, Aries," Mrs. Lexington muttered.

"That sounds like the god of war, doesn't it?" asked Josh. Both Leonidas and his mother nodded. "Why doesn't it surprise me?"

"Ah, here we go!" exclaimed Mrs. Lexington. "Oh, this is very interesting."

"What does it say?" asked Leonidas eagerly.

"*Do not hold on to anything too tightly and trust your heart. For the next few days, the stars are aligned for indulgence. You should splurge on something frivolous, something completely unnecessary, but that you really want,*" read Mrs. Lexington. "Ooh, I wish that were mine. I'd love to get those new shoes I saw at the mall. Shall I read yours to you, Josh?"

"No, Mom." Josh was watching Leonidas, who was clearly deep in thought. "Does that mean we get to rest, Leo? I know it would be frivolous, but don't you really, really want to rest? Or how about we shut the window in my bedroom? That would be frivolous, too."

Leonidas was staring out the window. "I did not think to ask for it. I did not think it was possible, but now I know it is what I must do."

Oh, no, thought Josh. *Now we're really in for it.*

8 THE GLOVES ARE OFF!

"A fight song?" questioned Katie, puzzled.

"Yes." Leonidas nodded his head. "When we march into the gymnasium, we must terrify our enemy with our power. Our voices must be raised in song. It is always the way. You have such a command of words, Katie, that you must write it for us."

A smile flashed across Katie's face as he complimented her, but almost immediately she frowned again. "You're just trying to get me back on the team, aren't you?"

"Perhaps," said Leonidas. "But when I consulted the oracle, it told me to trust my heart. I do not know what I would do without you." He looked at her softly with his large brown eyes. Katie couldn't help herself. She sighed. He was just so good-looking.

"All right," she finally agreed. "What kind of fight song do you want?"

"Something truly terrible. A song to make our enemies gasp and flee in terror. A fighting song. A biting song."

"Wait a minute," interrupted Katie. "What has Josh been telling you?"

"Only what a fearsome soldier you are."

"Does Lizzie know about this?"

"No. Why should she?"

Now Katie really smiled. "No reason. I'm going to get to work on this right away." She jumped off the couch, grabbed her notebook and a pen, and headed upstairs.

"Do you see, Josh?" said Leonidas. "It is not so hard to handle girls after all."

"I'm not so sure," said Josh. Upstairs, he heard the phone ring. He figured Lizzie would know about the song by the end of the night. But he was wrong. She knew before dinner.

"Phone for you, Leonidas," called Mrs. Lexington from the kitchen just before six.

Leonidas jumped up from the rug where he and Josh had been doing sit-ups. "I am still not used to these phones. What a difference they would make in battle! You could send messages to your leader in an instant without having to rely on runners. They are truly a wonder."

Josh collapsed on the floor. "Do you ever think of anything besides war?" asked Josh.

"What else is there?" countered Leonidas. He walked into the kitchen to get the phone.

Just then, Katie ran downstairs with a piece of paper in her hand. "I've got the song!"

"Yeah," said Josh. "Who'd you tell you were writing it?"

"Just Kelley," said Katie. "Why do you ask?"

When Mrs. Lexington called everyone into dinner a few minutes later, Leonidas looked despondent. He was sitting at the table, his head in his hands.

"Lizzie found out?" said Josh.

"She says she needs absolute authority if she is to be commander. That she will decide if we need a fight song or not."

"Don't you want to hear my song?" pouted Katie.

Leonidas threw up his hands. "Why not?"

"You wrote a song, Katie?" said Mrs. Lexington. "How wonderful!" Both she and Mr. Lexington beamed.

"Thanks, Mom." Katie held up her lined notebook paper, cleared her throat, and began singing.

"Two, four, six, eight
Who we gonna mutilate?
Liquidate! Eviscerate! Decapitate!
The blood and guts are on the floor
We are going to win with gore. . . ."

As she continued, the song got more and more specific. Gradually, the smiles evaporated from Mr. and Mrs. Lexington's faces and were replaced by looks of horror. Josh's mouth was hanging open and his face had turned a pale shade of green. Leonidas's eyes were sparkling.

Katie raised a fist in the air and shouted, "Hurrah!" when she finished the song. "Think it will scare the other team?" she asked. Mr. and Mrs. Lexington both just nodded. They were speechless.

"I think I'm going to start locking my door at night," said Josh. "I can't believe you sleep down the hall from me. Yikes!"

"Did you write that yourself, honey?" said Mrs. Lexington weakly.

"Yeah. Leonidas wanted me to write something to freak out Morris Middle School."

"That'll do it!" said Mr. Lexington. "It sure freaked me out." He shuddered.

"You might want to have a teacher take a look at it first. Make sure it's appropriate. Okay, honey?" pleaded Mrs. Lexington. "I wouldn't want you to get in trouble."

"It is a wondrous song, Katie!" enthused Leonidas. He was looking at her in a whole new way — the way he had looked at Lizzie after their first dodgeball game together. "Your song is sure to inspire the troops. It must be sung. It must. Any girl in Sparta would be proud to have written such a song."

"I guess Greek girls are pretty tough," said Mr. Lexington, shaking his head.

"Spartan women give birth to real men. They must be warriors," explained Leonidas.

"I didn't realize everybody was in the army," said Mrs. Lexington, confused. "Is your mother in the army, too?"

"Everyone who isn't a slave must serve the state," said Leonidas.

"Slave?" said Mr. Lexington surprised. "You still have slaves?"

Joshua jumped in, ready as always to stop any conversation with a Time Flyer from becoming too revealing. "Yeah, Dad, don't you sometimes say you feel like you're a slave to the clock?"

"Well, that's true — I do," admitted Mr. Lexington.

"It's the same everywhere, Dad." Joshua raised his eyebrows at Leonidas, who immediately understood that he should drop the topic.

After they had done the dishes, all three kids went upstairs to Katie's room. "So you think Lizzie will like the song as much as you do?" asked Josh when the door was shut.

Leonidas sighed and clenched his fists. "I do not know what to do. We need both. We need Katie's mighty song and we need Lizzie's strength and cunning."

"But Lizzie told you she'll drop out and take her friends with her if you use it, right?" guessed Katie.

"Yes," acknowledged Leonidas. "This is all so confusing. I miss my brothers from the barracks. It is easy for us to work together. I am beginning to understand why we are on our own away from the girls."

Katie looked at Leonidas. "I thought you were tough. I thought you were going to make the secret police, maybe even be a general someday. You'd think you could at least manage Lizzie Markle.

How good a commander are you going to be if you can't manage one sixth-grade girl?"

"She is very difficult," said Leonidas.

"Tell me about it," said Katie. "But if your head is as strong as your body, you'll figure it out. Right?"

Leonidas paused, and then he reached over and clasped Katie's hand. "Right," he agreed. "I will bend Lizzie Markle to my will."

I can't wait to see this, thought Josh. *I just hope he knows what he's up against.*

9 DOWN FOR THE COUNT

The next morning, Lizzie stomped over to Leonidas's desk. "I heard that song at my locker," she hissed. "Everyone's already singing it. And it's disgusting. Just the kind of thing someone like Katie Lexington would write. You have to tell everybody we're not singing it. Now."

Leonidas leaned back in his chair. "But can you not see how it has raised everyone's spirits? Troops need a good song to unite and inspire them."

"Yeah?" said Lizzie. "Then I'll write you one. I used to be a cheerleader and I can make up something good."

But Leonidas was not impressed with what she handed him at recess. "There is nothing to make the blood of our enemies boil in these taunts. What is this 'rah, rah,' nonsense?" he said. "We will use Katie's song and we will discuss this matter no further."

Lizzie sat on the ground for the rest of the recess period. And at gym, she said she had a stomachache and went to the nurse.

The next day, a group of her friends joined her protest and refused to have anything to do with Leonidas's training program. "I guess we'll just have to lose the races and the dodgeball game," said Lizzie. "But at least you'll win for songwriting."

"Good work," said Josh to Leonidas. "You've really got this situation under control."

"Great warriors are always problematic," said Leonidas. "Even the famous Achilles refused to fight when he did not get his way."

"Yeah? Did they ever get him back in battle?"

"His best friend was speared to death. That got him out of his tent."

"Let's not try that here, okay?"

Leonidas nodded his head seriously. "It would work, but I will think of something else."

By that point, every kid in the school — except Lizzie Markle and her clique — was working out and more excited about the Winter Games than ever. Mr. Kilmer, however, still didn't like Leonidas. "Your shoelaces are untied, kid. Don't ever come into my gym with your shoes untied. You hear me?"

The morning before the games, Josh woke up, but Leonidas was nowhere to be found. He slammed the window shut — he went to bed in his hat and mittens these days — and came downstairs expecting to find Leonidas already at breakfast. But he wasn't there, either. "Have you seen Leo?" Josh asked Katie.

"No. I thought he must be sleeping in. Leonidas wasn't due to go back yet, was he?" Katie asked her mother.

"I don't know. I never seem to know. It's really one of the biggest problems with Time Flyers. I love the children, but the program itself is so mismanaged . . . never knowing when the children are arriving or leaving, always showing up without a suitcase. Now if I were running it . . ."

On the bus to school Josh kept looking out the

window, hoping to catch sight of Leonidas running along on the sidewalk, but even though there were plenty of kids jogging to school these days, he didn't see any long-haired Spartans. When the bus finally pulled up in front of the school, Josh and Katie spotted Leonidas in the glass-enclosed office — with Mr. Kilmer.

"He's wearing his red cloak," said Josh. "Does he have anything else on?"

"I can see sneakers and, yup, blue jeans." Katie breathed a sigh of relief.

"Look at the way Kilmer's got him by the arm. You don't suppose they caught him stealing stuff from people's houses, do you?"

"Oh, no!" said Katie. "He's not still doing that, is he? I thought he'd stopped. He ate some mashed potatoes last night."

"Well, there was a plate of fresh chocolate chip cookies underneath the bed yesterday that I don't think Mom made. I can see the headlines NOW: NAKED BANDIT IS REALLY TIME-TRAVELING ANCIENT GREEK. We're gonna be in supermarkets all across the country," moaned Josh.

"Wow! Kilmer's really yelling at him. Can you tell what he's saying?"

At that moment, their mother appeared. "I got a call from the school just after you got on the bus and rushed here as fast as I could. This is just terrible. Terrible."

Mr. Walsh, the principal, came out of the office as soon as he saw Mrs. Lexington. "Thank you for coming over so quickly. We are all very upset, as you can imagine — and we'd like to keep this out of the papers."

"Newspapers? What's going on?" insisted Katie. "Is anybody going to tell us?"

"I've called Animal Control," Mr. Walsh was saying to Mrs. Lexington as he led her into the office. Josh and Katie quickly followed before he could shut the door.

"Animal Control?" whispered Josh.

"That's weird," Katie whispered back.

"My gym is a mess!" Mr. Kilmer screamed at Leonidas as they came into the office. "Dog poop everywhere! I want you to clean it up, young man. How am I going to get those floors repolished

86

before the Winter Games tomorrow? What kind of crazy prank was this? Did someone from Morris Middle School put you up to this?"

Leonidas was staring defiantly at Mr. Kilmer. "It is precisely for the benefit of your Winter Games that I brought the dogs to the battlefield. We must appease the gods of Mount Olympus. I only regret that I could not find any goats or black bulls."

"Everybody, slow way down," said Mr. Walsh, raising his hands. "Let's all take a seat and see if we can get to the bottom of this situation. Young man, do you want to try explaining yourself again?"

"Certainly, sir." Leonidas bowed toward Mr. Walsh.

"I just want to know who's cleaning up the dog poop!" growled Mr. Kilmer again.

"Calm down, Hank," said Mr. Walsh sternly. "Leonidas?"

"I have been concerned," began Leonidas, "that we have made no plans for appropriate sacrifices before the games. If we do not spill the blood of the beasts and offer up their thigh bones, will the gods not seek revenge upon us and spill *our* blood?"

Nobody knew what to say. Josh groaned. He could already see the photographers outside their house snapping pictures of their crazed, dog-sacrificing time traveler.

"I'm not sure I understand this," said Mr. Walsh finally, loosening his tie. "You wanted to, let me get this right, *sacrifice* these dogs in the gymnasium?"

"I've been telling you all month that this kid's a foreign freak!" boomed Mr. Kilmer.

"Calm down, Hank," Mr. Walsh repeated. "Let's just try and get a handle on this. We have to be sure to respect everyone's religious differences. Were you going to kill the dogs, young man?"

"Once we had created the appropriate altar and lit the sacramental fires, yes, of course," said Leonidas. "I realize dogs are a poor substitute for goats or bulls, but I did try to find mostly black ones."

Mrs. Lexington gasped. "You were going to

kill little doggies?" She reached out an arm and clasped Katie to her protectively.

"I think it's something they do in Greece. Don't worry about it so much, Mom," said Katie. "Leonidas, we don't do that here. Okay? You should have checked with us."

"I guess people do have different customs," said Mrs. Lexington weakly. "That's why we're doing this program, to learn about how people from all over the world live. I mean, I have heard that in some countries people even eat dogs."

"Well, kid, listen to me," barked Mr. Kilmer. "We don't do that here in America. No siree."

"All the dogs are fine, right?" said Josh desperately. Mr. Walsh nodded. "And someone from Animal Control can get them back to their homes, right?" Mr. Walsh nodded again. "So there isn't any harm done?"

"No harm done? Have you seen my gym? There were fifteen dogs in there all morning marking their territory."

Mr. Walsh stood up. "You're right, Josh. All the dogs are fine, and this situation is under control." He glared at Mr. Kilmer. "However, I think Leonidas needs to accept responsibility for his actions and help the janitor clean up the gym this morning."

"Certainly, sir," said Leonidas crisply. "I apologize for not anticipating and following the rules. I will accept your punishment. But do allow me to recommend perhaps the sacrifice of just one animal. I would hate to see Alice R. Quigley lose the games tomorrow."

"That's it!" shouted Mr. Kilmer. "I don't want this kid on my team. He doesn't even go to this school full-time."

Josh leaped up. "You can't do that, Mr. Kilmer. He's our only hope! Morris Middle School has some new star athlete! The kid's amazing! Leonidas is the only one who can beat him."

"My students are just as good as any foreigners. I want that kid off my team."

Leonidas's face was stony, but Katie noticed that he was clenching and unclenching his fists.

Mr. Walsh looked at each of them in turn. "I'm sorry, kids," he said finally. "I think Mr. Kilmer has a point. This was a pretty serious violation of school policy. Leonidas, you can attend the Games tomorrow with your classmates. But you may not participate. Now, why don't you head down to the gym and give Mr. Conway a hand with the cleanup?"

Leonidas stood up and bowed to them all. "I will respect the customs of your country."

"He was our only chance to win," said Josh to Katie when they were alone in the hall, walking back to class. "Morris has a superhero athlete, and we don't have Leonidas or even Lizzie. We're going to lose the Games for sure. This has been a disaster. I knew we should have gotten a ninja. They operate on their own. They come in, do what they're supposed to, and leave. They're trained assassins. That's what we needed. You should have listened to me."

And for once, Katie agreed with Josh.

10 THE FINISH LINE

At recess, everyone crowded around Leonidas. Josh had spread the word that Mr. Kilmer didn't want Leonidas on the team because of permission slip problems. "Keep quiet about the dogs," Josh had ordered him.

"Kilmer is such a pain," said Neil. "Now we'll never win. And no one will get an A this term."

"It is not about the grade," insisted Leonidas. "You can still prove yourselves. You can still try out for my secret team."

"Is it still on?" asked Frank and Evan.

"Of course it is," said Leonidas. "And I will be watching everyone's performance at the Games tomorrow. For that, it is actually better that I am not participating."

That afternoon, Leonidas grabbed Josh just as he was about to get on the bus. "Are we not going to jog home as usual?"

"What's the point?" said Josh, slinging his backpack over his shoulder.

Leonidas's eyes glittered. "The point is that the success of tomorrow's Games now depends entirely on your leadership. The gods are not with us. I cannot play. Lizzie chooses not to play. You alone must lead Alice R. Quigley to victory against Morris Middle School."

"How am I going to do that?" asked Josh.

"Your training will show," said Leonidas. "And as my mother has always said to me, 'You will come home carrying your shield or dead upon it.'"

"Great," said Josh. "That's just great."

The morning of the Games was icy cold and clear. Everyone ate hurriedly, packed their gym clothes in their backpacks, and hurried to the bus. Leonidas had said they must not waste energy before the competition. "You must all gather in the gym as soon as everyone has changed and sing the fight song to rally the troops," he told Josh and Katie. "I will be in the stands cheering you to victory."

Parents and teachers from both schools filled the stands. Lizzie sat as far away from Leonidas as she could. The art class had made banners that hung across the ceiling. Mr. Kilmer was stomping around the room with his grade book in one hand and a spray bottle of disinfectant in the other. The kids from Morris Middle School all came into the gym with their teacher and took seats near the climbing wall. When they entered, Leonidas stood up in his seat, clearly startled by something. He called out Josh's name, but Josh was still in the locker room. He was headed out of his seat when Mrs. Pitney pulled him back. Leonidas took his seat, but tapped his hands against the wooden bench. He was obviously agitated.

Mr. Kilmer banged on the doors to each of the locker rooms. "Time to come out and win!" he shouted to his students. But for a moment, no one appeared. Then, suddenly, all the boys and girls burst out, marching in formation and singing Katie's fight song at the top of their lungs. "*Two, four, six, eight! Who we gonna mutilate?*"

At first, all the parents and teachers cheered along with the students. But one by one, as they listened to the words of the song, everyone in the stands fell silent except Leonidas. *Did they really say "decapitate"?* Mrs. Pitney muttered to herself. A couple of the kids from Morris Middle School looked genuinely scared. Mr. Walsh ran over to Mr. Kilmer and began whispering something urgently to him, but Mr. Kilmer looked like he had no idea what he was talking about. Finally, Mr. Walsh stepped up to the microphone as the kids linked hands, raised them in the air, and shouted, "Hurrah!" one last time.

"Well, well, that was some song. We'll have to find out who wrote that." Mr. Walsh laughed nervously. "I wouldn't take it too seriously, folks. I mean today is about fun and games, after all."

As Mr. Walsh welcomed the competitors and described the upcoming events, Leonidas slipped out of his seat and ran over to where Josh was standing. He took him by the arm and pulled him aside. "You are in great danger," he whispered.

"I know that," said Josh. "Why are you telling me that now?"

"Do you see that boy over there?" He pointed to a particularly muscular sixth grader from Morris Middle School.

"That's the kid I was telling you about!" said Josh. "He's amazing."

"I know," said Leonidas. "He nearly beat me at the Olympics last year."

"What?" Josh was stunned.

"Hippolytus is from Athens."

"Hippolytus! That's his name!"

"He is a ruthless competitor."

"You mean to tell me someone from Morris Middle School has a Time Flyer, too?"

"It must be so. There can be no mistaking his name and face. You must watch Hippolytus in the dodgeball game. I have seen him throw the discus, and he has tremendous power. How I wish that I could go up against him. You must destroy him for me, Josh. You must."

Mr. Kilmer blew his whistle and grabbed the microphone from Mr. Walsh. "Let the Games begin!" he announced.

First up was the fifty-yard dash. Katie took off like lightning and easily won first place in the girls' race. She flashed Leonidas an enormous smile. Josh took his place on the starting line a moment later. Right beside him was the Athenian Time Flyer. "I'm not scared of you," Josh whispered to him before the whistle. "You didn't even win at the Olympics." Hippolytus was stunned by Josh's comment and hesitated for a moment after the whistle. Josh managed to cross the finish line just before him. "You distracted me like a Spartan," he said to Josh. "But you better watch yourself in dodgeball."

In the other races, Alice R. Quigley was also bringing home the gold. Neil Carmody was thrilled to find himself the champion of the long jump, and the overweight fifth grader Josh had sat with weeks ago at lunch was now noticeably leaner and climbing the ropes faster than anyone from either school.

"We're ahead!" said Katie to Josh at halftime.

"Yeah, but we've still got the dodgeball game. And that kid's from ancient Greece, too," said Josh, pointing at Hippolytus.

"Really?" said Katie.

"He knows Leonidas."

Lizzie, her entire body tense, had been jumping up and down during each of the matches, yelling at the girls even louder than Mr. Kilmer. "Don't hold back, Vanessa," she shouted. "Go for it!" As everyone took their places for the dodgeball game, she became frantic. "You guys need to do a dance as a warm-up! Work together. Watch each other," she shouted. "Don't forget what I taught you!"

Mr. Kilmer and the gym teacher from Morris Middle School placed the red gym balls along the center line. Josh crouched over, ready to leap forward. Hippolytus was right in front of him. Josh hurled his whole body forward as the whistle blew and grasped a ball. It flew out of his hands, but Hippolytus nimbly arched his back and avoided it. A moment later, Hippolytus grabbed another ball and whipped it toward a distracted Laurie. As she jumped out of the way, she slammed into Vanessa, knocking her down. Mr. Kilmer blew his whistle and shouted, "Time out!"

He and the other gym teacher rushed over to Vanessa and helped her to her feet. Vanessa was holding her head and seemed unable to stand without assistance. In the meantime, Lizzie Markle had run down from the stands and was talking urgently to Mr. Walsh. "I'm still on the list, aren't I?" Josh heard her say. "I'll take Vanessa's place."

"Glad to have you back on board," said Josh as Lizzie took her place beside him.

"There's no way you'll win without me," said Lizzie.

"Probably not," said Josh. "Can you help me take out the guy who tried to knock out Laurie?"

"Happy to," said Lizzie. "But that doesn't mean your sister gets to be on my secret team after the Games."

"I don't think that'll be a problem," said Josh. "Watch out!"

Mr. Kilmer had blown his whistle, and balls were flying again. Other than Laurie, not a single kid from Alice R. Quigley had been struck out. Kids passed one another balls, worked together, and one by one took out every boy and girl on the other side. They moved together in formation like dancers. Soon the only person left from Morris Middle School was Hippolytus. Still no one seemed able to strike him out. He whipped ball after ball at them, leaping from one side of the gym to the other. But finally, his luck ran out. Josh, Katie, and Lizzie all held balls in their hands.

"Are you ready?" asked Josh.

"I'm ready," said Lizzie.

"Me, too," said Katie, and all three let their balls fly at Hippolytus at the exact same moment.

No matter which way he moved, he'd be hit. And he knew it. *Boom! Boom! Boom!* They all hit him one after the other, and a great, roaring cheer erupted from everyone on Alice R. Quigley's team.

Hippolytus raised his arm in a salute to Josh, Lizzie, and Katie. "I acknowledge the champions," he said.

Leonidas had run down from the stands. "You did it! You all did it!" he was shouting. Everyone was high-fiving him and slapping him on the back.

"We couldn't have done it without you," said Frank.

"Did I make the team?" asked Neil.

"You *all* made the team!" said Leonidas. "You already *are* a team! Look at how you played. You are all amazing!"

"I can't believe it," said Mr. Kilmer. "We finally won the Winter Games. But that doesn't mean you all get an A. I saw some untied shoelaces out there."

"He is a very tough trainer," Hippolytus said to Leonidas.

"He would not let us sacrifice before the games," said Leonidas.

"I had the same problem at my school."

Josh came up beside Leonidas. "I just want to say thank you. You really got us all in shape. You're going to make a great commander someday."

"Yeah," said Katie. "I only wish you could have played with us. But at least we can all work out together tomorrow."

"I am afraid not, Katie." Leonidas reached up for the hourglass necklace around his neck. "It is just about time for me to return to my own country."

"Me, too!" said Hippolytus. "We can travel together." Around his neck was a matching hourglass necklace. The sand had nearly run through it.

"Wait just one minute," said Leonidas. "Mr. Kilmer!"

"What is it, kid?"

"I just wanted to extend my congratulations to you and invite you to visit Sparta someday."

"I learned all I need to know about your country yesterday cleaning up dog poop."

"Oh, I don't think you know anything about my country at all." Leonidas looked over at Hippolytus and nodded, and the next moment they both touched their hourglass necklaces. Later on, some of the kids said they'd seen a flash of blue light, and others remembered a sonic boom, but everyone was too busy congratulating one another and running around the gym to notice Leonidas and Hippolytus disappear — everyone, that is, except Josh, Katie, and Mr. Kilmer.

"Whoa!" yelled Mr. Kilmer. "Holy gamoley! What was that!"

"What was what?" asked Josh.

"I didn't see anything," said Katie. "Are you okay, Mr. Kilmer?"

Mr. Kilmer was slapping the side of his head. He whirled around. "They disappeared into thin air! You know they did. Tell me what happened now, or you both get Fs!"

"What are you talking about, Hank?" asked Mr. Walsh, coming over. "Are you messing with these kids' grades again? I'm getting pretty tired of this. I've had too many parents calling my office this year."

"You're in on it, aren't you? You're *all* in on it!"

"In on what?" asked Mr. Walsh, concerned.

He started to take Mr. Kilmer by the arm, but Mr. Kilmer pulled away.

"Those foreign kids! I knew there was something strange about them! They evaporated like . . . like aliens! There's no way I'm passing that kid. If he wants his credits transferred, he's in for a big surprise."

"Now, Hank, let's all calm down. It's been a stressful day. I'm sure they're just in the locker room. You didn't see anything, kids, did you?" asked Mr. Walsh, turning to Josh and Katie.

"Not a thing," said Josh.

"Nope. Not a thing," said Katie.

"I bet it was some secret military experiment," muttered Mr. Kilmer, rubbing his eyes. "That would explain everything."

EPILOGUE: PASSING THE TORCH

"You know, I had my doubts about Leonidas, but he was our best Time Flyer ever," said Josh.

It was snowing so hard outside that school had been canceled, and Mr. and Mrs. Lexington couldn't get to work. Everyone was still in their pajamas around the kitchen table. "He was a very polite boy," said Mrs. Lexington. "But he did have some odd habits."

"I guess," said Katie. "But we couldn't have won the Winter Games without him."

"But he didn't even run any races or play dodgeball," said Mrs. Lexington.

"He didn't have to," said Josh. "He showed us

how to. I sure hope he gets to be a commander someday."

"Anyone heard where Mr. Kilmer's gone?" said Mr. Lexington, looking up from the newspaper.

"They mentioned at the last PTA meeting that he'd taken an extended leave of absence," said Mrs. Lexington. "Mr. Walsh seemed to feel he was a little worn out. He mentioned something about hallucinations."

"Did he?" said Josh.

"That's strange," said Katie, not daring to look at her brother.

"How's the new gym teacher?" asked their father.

"He's really nice," said Josh.

"Yeah," said Katie. "We're doing square dancing."

"Ugh!" shuddered Mr. Lexington. "I used to hate dancing in gym."

"Really?" said Josh. "Leonidas told us it was the best way to learn teamwork."

"Is that so?"

"Yup," said Katie. "It's not as bad as I used to think it was."

"Do you think you'll get an A this term?" asked her mother.

"I think everyone will get an A," said Katie.

"But you know what?" said Josh. "We earned it."

BACK WITH LEONIDAS IN ANCIENT SPARTA: 450 B.C.

Today you are out gathering rushes to weave a bed for yourself. You are not allowed blankets or a mattress at the *agōgē*, the military academy you attend. The rough grasses cut your hands as you pull them up, but at least a mat gives you some protection from the bare ground. The wind blows, and you pull your red cloak closer around you. It is the only article of clothing you are allowed. You live on the peninsula that will one day be known as Greece, but you consider yourself a citizen of Sparta, a city that needs no walls because its soldiers are so powerful. You are training to be one of those soldiers.

Family Life

When you are born, a council of elders arrives to decide your fate. If you are deformed or weak, you will be placed out on a hillside to die. Only the strong are allowed to live. Sometimes, however,

abandoned babies are rescued by childless couples or slave dealers.

Until you are seven, you will live with your family. Your father does not share meals with you. He belongs to an eating club with his warrior friends. If he is still a young man, he does not even sleep at your house, but remains in the barracks with the other soldiers. Your mother, who has more rights than most women in the ancient world, runs the household. In Spartan fashion, your home is kept simple. No one believes in showing off their wealth or adding any extra adornment or comfort to their surroundings.

School

You are training to be a warrior and you learn to read, write, dance, and sing because all of these skills will help you become a better fighting machine. Older boys supervise the training of the younger ones, and the discipline is rigorous. You are beaten a lot. You are given very little to eat and are expected to develop cunning by stealing your food. However, if anyone catches you, you will be brutally punished — for being foolish enough to get caught.

The year before you become a man, you will be sent off to fend for yourself. At the end of this time, you will return for an initiation ceremony at the temple of Artemis, where you and other boys

"Mom, I got an A! I survived!"

of your age will be whipped until your blood flows across the goddess's altar. Some boys will die during this ceremony, but your parents will cheer you on as you prove yourself to be a mighty warrior.

Girls

One day, your sister will grow up to be the mother of a warrior. For this she, too, needs to be trained like a soldier. Unlike many cultures in the ancient world, she is given as much food as you are so that she will grow up strong. Visitors are

"Boy, it's hard work learning how to be a mom!"

surprised by how tall and beautiful the Spartan girls are. This may have something to do with how much they get to eat!

When she becomes an adult, your sister will actually be allowed to own property in her own name and decide who she would like to be the father of her children. When she eventually dies, if she is a mother, she will be given the same honor as a fallen warrior — a gravestone with her name on it.

The Gods and Goddesses

The whole natural world is controlled by the gods and goddesses. As Apollo drives his chariot across the sky, the sun rises and sets. While there are twelve major gods and goddesses who live on Mount Olympus, there are tons of lesser deities who rule over particular places.

The gods and goddesses are jealous, angry, vengeful, and difficult. It's usually a good idea to know what they think before you do anything so

you don't make them even angrier. You consult oracles, divine priests, and priestesses who live in special temples, to speak with them for you. The oracles often give you mysterious sayings, which you may or may not interpret correctly. Sometimes the priests will study the insides of sacrificed animals to get a sense of the future. It's like reading palms. Sort of.

The Big Twelve

Zeus — the king, the lightning bearer
Hera — the queen
Athena — the goddess of wisdom and, surprise,
          Athens
Hermes — the messenger and god of travelers
Poseidon — the god of the sea
Ares — the god of war
Aphrodite — the goddess of love
Hades — the god of the underworld
Artemis — the goddess of the hunt and young
          women
Apollo — the god of the sun
Hephaestus — the blacksmith god
Hestia — the goddess of the hearth and home

The Trojan War

It's a long story. Ten years long.

Three goddesses — Hera, Athena, and Aphrodite — asked Paris, a prince of Troy, which of them was the prettiest. They all tried to bribe him. Hera promised him power, Athena promised him wealth, and Aphrodite promised him the most beautiful woman in the world. Paris chose Aphrodite, and his reward was Helen of Sparta. Unfortunately, Helen was already married. Her husband, Menelaus, his brother, Agamemnon, and all the Greek warriors, including the famous Achilles, fought the Trojans for ten years to get her back from Troy. Finally, the Greeks tricked the Trojans by giving them a big horse in which their whole army was hiding. Surprise!

You listen to this story a lot. It's filled with exciting battles, descriptions of weapons, and all kinds of military lore. It's already an old story in your day. Eventually, it will be written down and called *The Iliad*.

The First Olympics

The very first Olympics are held in 776 B.C. in honor of the king of the gods — Zeus. Originally a local religious festival, it has become a major event held every four years where athletes from

all the Greek city-states compete against one another. With its well-trained warriors, Sparta is often triumphant.

On the first day, all the men and boys get together to make the appropriate sacrifices and hold religious ceremonies. No women or girls are allowed to either compete or watch, although they do have their own footrace in honor of Hera, the queen of the gods. The races begin on the second day. All the competitors are naked and barefoot — maybe that's why the girls aren't allowed in! In the beginning, there are just running races, but every year new events are added — wrestling, chariot races, discus throwing. The winner of each contest gets a crown of olive leaves (not a gold medal) and there are no second- or third-place prizes. Winner takes all!

ABOUT THE AUTHOR

Perdita Finn lives in the Catskill Mountains with her husband (a runner), two children (swimmers), five cats (mousers), and a long-haired dachshund who really needs to get in shape.